Book IV

Minokichi

BOOK IV

Minokichi

Novelization by John Whitman
Based on the teleplay by Tom Szollosi

BANTAM BOOKS

New York · Toronto · London · Sydney · Auckland

RL: 5.5, AGES 10 and up

MINOKICHI

A Bantam Skylark Book / May 2003

All rights reserved.
Text copyright © 2003 by Mind's Eye International, Inc.
Cover art copyright © 2003 by Mind's Eye International, Inc.

ISBN 0-553-48762-0 (pbk.)
0-553-13027-7 (lib. bdg.)

**Visit us on the Web! www.randomhouse.com/kids
Educators and librarians, for a variety of teaching tools,
visit us at www.randomhouse.com/teachers**

Published simultaneously in the United States and Canada

Bantam Skylark is an imprint of Random House Children's
Books, a division of Random House, Inc. SKYLARK BOOK
and colophon and BANTAM BOOKS and colophon are
registered trademarks of Random House, Inc.

PRINTED IN THE UNITED STATES OF AMERICA

10 9 8 7 6 5 4 3 2 1

Chapter One

Lily Bellows tried to escape from the day-to-day world by cooking, but it didn't work.

She closed the oven with a sigh. It was no use. Everything she did reminded her of her husband. Dr. Matt Bellows, an archaeologist who was an expert in mythology, had vanished a few weeks ago, leaving behind his frightened and bewildered family. Since that day, Lily had spent most of her time worried sick about him, and even when she tried to keep busy, she found herself reminded of his work. Myths and folklore, as

Matt had told her many times, surround us. They influence the way we think and act even when we don't realize it—even in the kitchen. For thousands of years, people said blessings over their food. When cooks spilled salt, they tossed a bit over their shoulders to ward off evil.

Lily frowned. Too late for her. Evil had already come . . . and somehow it had taken her husband away.

The doorbell rang, calling Lily back to the present. Wiping her hands on a dish towel, she walked down the hall to the door and opened it. The man standing there had white hair and a white beard trimmed to look as neat and clean as his tweed blazer. Despite his white hair, his straight back and bright eyes made him look much younger than his sixty-five years. He carried a small box in his hand, and on his face he wore the smile of an old friend.

"Max Asher!" Lily said, both startled and pleased. "What are you doing here? Come in, please!" She threw her arms around the older man, then drew him into the house.

"Hi, Lily," he said.

"I thought you were still in Boston."

Max Asher nodded. "I just got back. I wanted to see you first thing." He looked at her

2

with a concerned expression. "How are things going?"

Lily shrugged. Max was one of her husband's oldest and most trusted friends and his mentor in archaeology. Of course he would have heard that Matt had vanished. Despite her sadness, she put on a brave face. "I barely have time to catch my breath these days. The kids are back in school, my catering business is busier than ever, and get this, I even have my own cooking show on the local cable channel."

She led him into the kitchen, where she was preparing a meal for one of her catering clients. Max smiled. "I'm jealous. Now everyone will get to taste your Indian quail."

Lily laughed. "I'll tell you what—I'll save the quail for you. In fact, you're just in time for lunch."

Max put a gentle hand on her arm. "Lily, thanks, but I'm not here to eat."

"What's this about, Max?" Lily asked, although she already knew. There was only one thing anyone wanted to talk to her about.

Max rubbed his beard for a moment, then said, "I was talking to Barbara Frazier. . . ."

"Oh, Max, not you too," Lily groaned, feeling her excitement suddenly drain away. Barbara

Frazier was a junior colleague who had worked in the university's archaeology department with Matt. When Matt disappeared, Barbara had become his chief accuser, suggesting that he had found something of immense value inside the mysterious Ch'ang-o statue and run off with it. Barbara was the main reason the police now thought of Lily's missing husband as a criminal. "Please say you're not here to tell me Matt was a thief. I thought you were his friend."

"Lily, I want to show you something." Max sat down and opened the box he was carrying. Inside sat a small lump of plastic shaped like a stone, about the size of a child's fist. The stone had been pierced by what looked like an arrow, or maybe a spear.

"What's this?"

Max said, "Well, you recall that when your husband disappeared, all anyone could find was an ancient Chinese statue that had been shattered."

"Right, the Ch'ang-o," Lily remembered. It was a jade piece that Matt had been studying. Shards of the priceless statue had been found scattered across the floor of Matt's study after he disappeared.

"And you know that the university reconstructed the Ch'ang-o and discovered—"

"That it was lighter than it had been before," Lily interrupted. "As though something had been taken from inside it. As though my husband had broken the statue open, stolen something hidden inside, and then run off. Yes, of course I know. That's all I've heard over and over from the university and from the police."

Max nodded and held up the plastic model. "This is a replica of what was inside that statue. The scan of the statue showed a space forming this shape exactly. I had it made once the statue was reconstructed."

Lily looked at the model. It was a strange-looking piece, but that wasn't unusual. From years of looking over Matt's shoulder while he worked, she knew there were thousands of ancient and very odd-looking sculptures from all over the world. But this one seemed familiar to her somehow. "You think it might have something to do with Matt's disappearance?"

"That's what I'm trying to find out."

Suddenly a wave of recognition swept across Lily's face. "Come with me," she said.

Lily led Max into her husband's study—a

high-ceilinged room filled with ancient artifacts collected over years of study in every part of the world. She opened an antique armoire and riffled through some papers before pulling out an old piece of parchment. "Remember when we were on that dig in Tibet in 1985? Matt was running one of the first expeditions through Changthang and I was studying the local cuisine. One day we were rummaging through a local market, and Matt found some parchments. Nobody in the town knew where they had come from, but Matt saw them as a find. He blew our food budget for the next week to buy them."

Asher chuckled. "That sounds like our Matt."

"Doesn't it? Anyway, this was the one he was most excited about."

Lily unrolled the parchment. It was covered with mystical symbols strung together into a creepy antique script. In the center of the writing, there was an image of a black stone with a spearhead thrust through the middle. More symbols were drawn along the length of the spearhead.

To Lily, the writing around the edges of the parchment was just gibberish, but as she watched

Max's eyes scanning it, she knew he could read it as if it were a part of the morning newspaper. With each movement of his eyes across the page, his brow wrinkled into a look of deeper and deeper concern.

Slowly, Max held up his plastic model. It looked exactly like the stone in the picture.

"Oh my God," Lily whispered after seeing the look on his face. "Max, is that what Matt found inside that thing? Is that why he's gone?"

Max couldn't take his eyes off the picture, but he nodded slowly and whispered, "I'm afraid it might be. Lily, I think Matt found the Gorgos Stone."

Chapter Two

Alex and Cleo Bellows traveled home from
school together, and together they carried an
enormous and unbelievable secret.

Neither one of them had to tell the other to
hurry home. Every afternoon when they got
there, they immediately went upstairs to their
father's study to continue their secret work.

Everyone in the city was searching for their
father, but only Alex, seventeen, and Cleo, two
years younger, knew where to look. And they
didn't tell anyone, because no one would have
believed them.

That was because the explanation was totally *un*believable. Alex and Cleo were convinced that their father had been sucked into the world of mythology through his computer system. The computer, which contained a record of almost every myth ever told, had somehow been transformed into a gateway to a world of myths and legends by a mystical object called the Gorgos Stone. Alex and Cleo were certain that their father was trapped somewhere among the hundreds of myths, and they were determined to get him back.

Reaching their house, Alex and Cleo entered through the kitchen door. As usual, Alex held the door open as Cleo rolled her wheelchair in, and, as usual, Cleo ran over his toes on purpose because she didn't like other people doing things for her.

They both cast a short "Hi, Mom" in their mother's direction, then went for the refrigerator. Alex and Cleo were anxious to get upstairs to continue the search for their father.

Lily looked up from a cookbook and said, "That's it? That's all I get? 'Hi, Mom,' and then you bury yourselves in the fridge?"

No response was heard except the sounds of containers being opened and food being devoured.

"How about telling me how your day at school was?" she added.

Alex shrugged. "Fine."

"What did you do?" Lily asked.

Cleo also shrugged. "Nothing."

Lily sighed. "Well, I'm so glad we've had this chance to talk."

Alex and Cleo nodded, loaded Cleo's lap with snacks, and turned away from the fridge. But they didn't make it out of the kitchen before their mother said, "Hold it. Before you two dive back into your homework, I have something to ask you."

Alex and Cleo stopped and waited.

"Max Asher visited me today," their mother said. "He showed me a model of something that came out of that statue your dad broke in the office."

Alex and Cleo looked at each other. Cleo spoke first, and she tried to sound surprised. "Out of the statue? What was it?"

Their mother held up the plastic model Max had left behind. Alex coughed. "Uh, why is Max worried about a piece of plastic?"

"This is just a model. The real thing is some kind of mythical relic called the Gorgos Stone."

"The Gorgos Stone?" Cleo asked innocently, as though she'd never heard of it before. But the truth was she *had* heard of it. And so had Alex. In fact, they knew far more about it than their mother did. But they had sworn to keep their activities a secret, even from their mom.

"What's a Gorgos?" Cleo added sweetly.

"I don't know," Lily confessed. "But your father was one of the few people who believed in its existence. Max thinks he was right after all."

"And Max doesn't know where the stone is now?" Alex asked cautiously.

"He's still trying to find out what could have happened to it—"

"—and if it had anything to do with Dad's disappearance," Alex concluded.

Their mother nodded, her face full of concern. "If your father was interested in it, there might have been other people interested too." She paused. She had started out wanting to explain to her children this new theory of their father's disappearance, but they weren't reacting the way she had expected. In fact, they reminded her of kids who had already peeked at their Christmas presents. She said, "Do you two know anything about it?"

Alex blinked. "Us? No." He looked at the piece of parchment on the table beside the plastic model. "But if I think of anything, I'll tell you. Anyway, I've got to get cracking on my homework. I'll see you later." Alex spun on his heel and sped out of the room.

Lily looked at her daughter. "What was that about?"

Cleo rolled her wheelchair a bit closer. "I don't know. I guess men start to make more sense as they get older, huh?"

Lily chuckled. "Don't hold your breath."

By the time Cleo had made a polite exit from the kitchen and used her special elevator to the second floor, Alex was already in their father's study, sitting at the desk and writing furiously.

"What was that all about?" Cleo asked. "You made Mom more suspicious. Why'd you run out like that?"

Alex kept his eyes on his work. "I wanted to get these down while they were fresh in my mind. They're the markings that were etched on that spearhead that was sticking through the stone. They might help us figure out where to find Dad."

"What is it?" Cleo asked. "Chinese?"

"Could be," her brother said. "Or maybe it's Japanese. The script is called Kanji."

Cleo was startled. "Since when did you become an Asian expert?"

Alex grinned. "Who says TV isn't educational? You can learn a lot from watching Japanese anime."

Alex spun his chair around and rolled over to the computer terminal. This was by far the most impressive part of the study. The setup was controlled by a small, high-tech laptop computer. Beside the laptop sat a high-fidelity microphone that allowed the user to enter voice commands, and a special scanner that scanned images in three dimensions. Mounted on the wall was a holographic plasma screen, a unique display unit that produced lifelike, three-dimensional images of whatever was scanned into the computer.

Alex scanned his drawing and watched the symbols appear on the laptop's screen. "If that stone has something to do with Dad disappearing into the myth world, then this writing is probably connected too."

"Connected to what?" Cleo asked.

"I don't know. Let's run it through the museum's search engine and see what it kicks out."

Cleo nodded. She loaded a program into the laptop and then spoke into the voice-command microphone. "Comparison search."

Instantly, the laptop's screen began to flicker as the computer sorted through thousands of images. Their father's computer was the gateway to a huge library of information stored both in their house and at the university's museum. Once he'd stopped traveling around the globe looking for ancient artifacts, their father had devoted his life to cataloging and storing them in an elaborate 3D archive called the CyberMuseum, where one could find virtual versions of every known artifact related to mythology.

After a full minute of searching, the screen froze on a single image. "Bingo," Cleo said. "It's from the Japanese room." She spoke into the microphone again. "Find artifact in Cyber-Museum."

This time they didn't look at the laptop. They looked up at the plasma screen on the wall. An image appeared there, floating and rotating in three dimensions. It was a beautifully designed woman's comb inlaid with a Kanji character.

"The comb is Japanese," Alex observed. "But the Ch'ang-o statue Dad left behind was Chinese. Do you think there's any connection?"

Cleo shrugged. "Maybe, especially since we found a Japanese symbol on the spearhead. It's the best lead we've had so far."

Alex stood up from the computer. "Exactly what I was thinking. Japan, here I come."

"You ready for another trip?" Cleo asked.

"Like I've got a choice," her brother said. He walked to the plasma screen and reached out, then hesitated. He hated this. But he couldn't give up searching for their father. With a quick glance over his shoulder and a weak smile, he said, "*Sayonara,* baby." Then he touched the image of the comb.

And vanished.

Chapter Three

There was a brief moment of being *between* places. Of being nowhere. Then, a fraction of a second later, Alex's stomach fell out the way it did when a roller coaster tipped down into a drop, and then his feet hit the ground with a suddenness that made his knees sting.

That was what teleportation to the Alterworld felt like. Alex had already been through it several times, and it didn't get any easier. Every image that he touched on the screen pulled him into some legend from somewhere in the world. His first trip had been to the Greece of myth, where he'd faced the half-man, half-bull creature called the Minotaur. The fact that the creature had never existed in the real world didn't matter—Alex hadn't gone back in time, he'd gone back into a mythological world . . . which meant anything was possible.

Now, as he recovered from the shock of transportation, Alex surveyed his surroundings. He was standing at the wooden gate of a small Japanese village. A thin layer of snow covered the ground, and a chilly wind seemed to blow right through him. He shivered.

"Brrr. It feels like Antarctica here. Why do I keep getting the cold myths?" he said out loud. One of his last adventures had drawn him into the snowy world of Norse mythology. "Don't they have any myths in Tahiti?"

Alex heard something squeak behind him. He turned and realized he was standing in the middle of a narrow lane that led up to the gate. An old woman was pulling a cart full of pots, pans, mirrors, beads, and other odds and ends. She smiled a gap-toothed smile at him, and he nodded. As she passed, Alex saw a reflection in one of the mirrors hanging from her cart. It was his face—or, at least, the face of the person he was in this myth. From the mirror, a young, friendly-looking Japanese woodcutter stared back at him. Looking at his own body, he would see himself as Alex, but everyone inside the myth would see him as he was in the mirror—as the character he had become.

"Well, this is definitely Japan," he said, smiling at his reflection.

"Alex!"

Cleo's voice popped out of the air. This was the only saving grace of his journeys to the Alterworld. Somehow, he could hear Cleo's voice when she spoke into the computer's voice-recognition system, and she could see him through the plasma screen. "The big question," she said. "How does this symbol connect to Dad's disappearance?"

"Minokichi!"

A voice called from the gate, and Alex turned to find a wizened old Japanese man staring at him. The old man's face was wrinkled and rough like the bark of a tree, but his black eyes twinkled like warm coals. There was an old woman, wearing an equally warm expression, standing beside him. Both were dressed in heavy coats to protect them from the cold, and Alex realized that he was wearing warm clothes too.

"Minokichi!" they called again, and Alex realized they were talking to him.

"Okay," he said quietly to himself, "I guess I'm Minokichi."

"We've got to go!" the old man said. "There are trees to cut."

"What do you think?" Alex whispered. Although no one in the Alterworld could hear Cleo, they could all hear him, and he didn't want anyone to think he'd gone crazy and started talking to the air.

Cleo replied, "At least he knows who you are. And that's more than we know right now."

"Nonsense," Alex muttered sarcastically. "I'm Minokichi and I cut trees. It all makes sense."

The man and woman motioned to him to move forward. The man pointed to the woman, who Alex figured must be his wife. "Noriko's packed us provisions. We have pieces of braised fish, ripe plums, and plenty of rice! We'll eat like kings as we work."

The woman chuckled. "If I left it to you, Mosaku, you'd starve out there. You'd leave me all alone, and then where would I be?"

Mosaku put his arm around her. "With no

19

one to drop wood shavings all over your clean floors." He grinned. "I couldn't bear to let that happen. You'd get bored."

He kissed her forehead, then turned to Alex. "Come, Minokichi. The trees are waiting, and I am not getting any younger."

He held out a pack, which Alex slung across his back. As the two men started out into the forest, snow began to fall, lightly at first, and then more heavily, but Mosaku kept walking.

They walked for several miles, each of which looked like the mile before it, until Alex finally said, "Excuse me, but aren't we supposed to be chopping wood or something? 'Cause I could swear these are trees we're passing."

Mosaku grinned again, his face wrinkling more deeply. "Of course these are trees, boy. Ordinary trees, which yield ordinary wood. And if you wish to be ordinary, you may cut them. But we're searching for something out of the ordinary."

Mosaku pointed ahead, somewhere behind the closest grove of trees. Alex could see a line of thin mist. "The mist marks the line of the river. Across it, we will find trees like no others. Richer grains, and the color is a deep red. People call them the Blood Trees."

Alex grimaced. "That can't be good. Nothing with *blood* in the name is ever good," he grumbled to himself.

Mosaku jabbed an elbow into his side and laughed. "Come along! Don't tell me you're not thinking of building a chest for your lady love!"

Alex hesitated. "I . . . don't think I have a lady love . . . do I?"

Mosaku shrugged. "Maybe it's because you haven't built a chest for her yet. Trust me."

Alex looked skeptical, which only made Mosaku laugh more loudly. "Trust me, Minokichi! I have a sense for these things. This trip will change your life."

The snow picked up, carried by a chill wind that moaned among the tree trunks. As their footsteps crunched the snow, Alex heard Cleo speak into his ear.

"Alex, I've been doing more research while you've been going for a hike. I can't find anything online about the Gorgos Stone. I'm going to do some checking downstairs."

"Hel-lo?" he whispered. "How about finding something about this myth I'm in? So far I'm chopping wood with this sweet old man, but I'm headed for Blood Trees, which I don't like the sound of at all, and I'm cold! I don't know

21

what I'll catch up with first—Dad, or a case of double pneumonia."

"Think warm thoughts. I'll be back."

He didn't bother arguing. There was nothing he could do while he was in the Alterworld, and his sister had a serious stubborn streak. She was going to do what she was going to do, with or without his consent. Instead of arguing, he pulled his coat tighter around his neck and leaned into the cold wind, following Mosaku's sloped shoulders as they pressed forward against the thickening snow. With every step the air grew colder and the wind blew harder. Soon it was so sharp that Alex felt as if someone was throwing panes of ice-cold glass into his face over and over again.

"Mosaku!" he yelled over the wind. "We can't go on like this!'

The old man glanced back over his shoulder. "No choice now. We're closer to the river than the village. We have to keep going!"

"What's at the river?"

"A ferryman's hut. Not elegant lodgings, but we can start a fire and keep ourselves warm."

That sounded promising. If they didn't find shelter soon, Alex was sure he would freeze, and he couldn't imagine that the old man was any warmer than he was.

"You're sure about this?" he asked.

"It's just ahead," Mosaku answered. "Trust me."

Then, with a startled cry, the old man disappeared.

Chapter Four

Alex blinked. One moment Mosaku had been standing in front of him, and the next he was gone. Alex took a step forward and felt his boot start to slip on the edge of the slanted pathway. He grabbed a tree branch to keep his footing and looked through the swirling snow. He squinted into the raging storm until he saw Mosaku lying on his back.

"Mosaku!" Alex shouted. He slid a few feet, then fell on his backside and body-sledded the rest of the way. He came to a stop beside the old woodcutter. "Are you all right?"

Mosaku winced and blinked once or twice. "Uh . . . I'm fine. I do that just to prove how well I bounce."

"You don't bounce very well."

"Perhaps I need more practice."

"*Less* practice might be healthier. Let me help you," Alex said as he lifted the old man to his feet. Mosaku had a nasty cut on his forehead. Blood trickled onto the snow, and the old cutter hastily kicked loose snow over it.

"Still want to keep going?" Alex asked.

Mosaku nodded, then said, "Look, I told you I'd find it." He pointed across a small, snowy field studded with bare trees. Through the driving snow, Alex saw the dark shape of a small building. "Come on, we have to get inside."

While Alex struggled through the snow, his sister wheeled herself into the kitchen of their house, where their mother was popping open Tupperware containers filled with food. Lily Bellows poured a heap of rice and chicken onto a plate.

"Wow, that smells good," Cleo said.

Her mother nodded with satisfaction. "Tastes even better. Tahini chicken with saffron rice. It's a new creation. You have to try it."

Cleo glanced up the stairs. She'd already been away from Alex for a short time, looking through books in their small family library. Another minute or two shouldn't matter, especially since all he seemed to be doing was walking in the woods. She tried a forkful of food. Warm spices melted in her mouth and she sighed. "Mmm, when you're right, you're right. This is great."

"Maybe we should get Alex down here too," her mother said.

Cleo tried not to look panicked. "Uh . . . I don't think so, Mom. Alex and tahini chicken aren't a good match. Unless it comes on a pizza or he can put ketchup on it, he's not interested."

Cleo must have looked as lame as her excuse, because her mom frowned and studied her for a moment in a way that only a mother could—a way that made Cleo want to spill her guts about every white lie she'd ever told. She bit her tongue instead.

"Cleo," her mother said after a moment, "is Alex all right?"

"Alex?" Cleo repeated nervously. "Sure. I mean, why do you ask?"

Lily poked at the chicken thoughtfully,

eventually taking a bite. "I don't know. He was just so jumpy before. He ran out of here like I'd handed him a frilly apron and asked him to do the dishes." She heaved a sigh. "I must admit, I was looking forward to your father dealing with the teenage boy issues."

"Mom, I don't think Alex *has* issues. . . ."

"You never know. Boys don't communicate. He could be having problems in school. He could even be in love."

"Alex?" Cleo asked, genuinely shocked. Her brother wasn't bad-looking, and he did have his own circle of friends . . . but he wasn't exactly considered the coolest kid in school. Alex and *girls*?

"Yes!" her mother replied, laughing. "He's a young man. It happens. And when it does . . . *Bam!* It's as if whatever was going on in your head just stops dead."

Cleo rolled her eyes. "Mom, Alex is a bit like that all the time."

Her mother sighed. "You have a point."

Meanwhile, Alex and Mosaku were huddled over a tiny fire inside a small, barren ferryman's hut at the edge of a frozen river. The wind howled outside, and now and then a cold gust blew into the room, chilling their bones and threatening to extinguish their fragile flame.

Mosaku had managed to light the fire using flint and tinder. It had not been easy. The old man had squatted over a pile of dry grass and twigs, striking the flint against a piece of metal, trying to make enough sparks to ignite the kindling.

What I wouldn't give for a match, Alex thought. *Or a space heater.*

Miraculously, a spark shot from the flint and lit a tiny tuft of dry grass, then began to smoke. Now the thin flames leaped and cracked over a small pile of twigs. The two men leaned close over the flame, for warmth and to protect it from the wind. Mosaku had taken two small wooden bowls and a sack of cooked rice from his backpack and divided the food between them. Alex dipped his fingers into the bowl and carefully put the rice into his mouth.

"Mmm," he sighed. "I never knew a bowl of plain rice could taste so good."

The old woodcutter nodded. "Everything tastes better when you cheat death, Minokichi. Of course," he added with a twinkle in his eye, "the night is long . . . and there is always the Yuki-onna. . . ."

Alex looked up from his meal. "And, um, what would the Yuki-onna be?"

Mosaku grinned like a grandfather being asked to tell a story from his childhood for the thousandth time. He hunkered down closer to the fire, its light flickering up to glow on his wrinkled face as he began to speak in a low voice.

"The Yuki-onna is the scourge of the Blood Forest," he began. "She's an ice demon, a creature of the cold who floats through the trees like a wraith, stalking travelers, hungry for their warmth—and their blood. Then, with a terrifying shriek, she swoops down to kill, freezing her prey with fear and drinking her fill!"

He lunged toward Alex, who jumped back despite himself and nearly choked on a mouthful of rice. "Uh, that's great, just great. I love old ghost stories."

Mosaku shook his head grimly. "Who said it was a story? They say that when the Yuki-onna spills the blood of her victims, the roots of the trees drink it up. That's why the wood is red. And that's why you can hear the trees moan in the wind. They're crying with the voices of the dead."

As he finished speaking, the wind picked up, howling through the forest outside and battering the walls of the little hut. Maybe it was just the story that Mosaku had told, but to Alex, the wind now sounded like the voice of a bitter and angry woman.

"That . . . that *is* just the wind, right?" he asked, suddenly hoping the door was locked.

Mosaku's face settled into a frightened mask. Then, in an instant, the mask was broken by the bright, mischievous eyes of a prankster. "Of course it is!" The old woodcutter erupted in laughter, slapping his knee and wiping a tear from his eye. "Ha, ha, ha! You like that, eh? Good story, huh?"

"Oh, yeah. Har, har, har," Alex mumbled sarcastically. "Top-notch."

Mosaku yawned. "Well, we should get some rest now. We can take turns sleeping."

"Take . . . take turns? But I thought you said it was just a story."

Mosaku laughed. "So we don't freeze! I wouldn't want this to be the last place I see."

Alex nodded and offered to sit up first. Mosaku happily agreed. The old man pulled his clothes tightly around himself, then curled around the fire. In moments, he was asleep.

For a long time Alex remained alert. At home, a ghost story of the Yuki-onna wouldn't have bothered him at all. But this wasn't home. It wasn't even really ancient Japan. This was the Alterworld, and that meant that ancient myths were real. He'd met gods and monsters on previous journeys . . . so the idea of running into an ice demon wasn't so far-fetched.

Now and then the wind hit the front of the hut, rattling the door so hard it nearly came off its hinges. Each time, Alex's heart froze as he imagined someone outside gripping the handle and shaking it. But no one ever entered. And after a while, the rattling took on a slow, steady rhythm that lulled him into a relaxed watchfulness. Then the cold set in, making him bundle up more tightly and edge closer to the fire. His eyes grew heavy and his chin dipped toward his chest.

The wind rattled the door again once, twice, three times—and then the door flew open and snow swirled into the room. But instead of swirling down and settling over the two sleepers, it spiraled up toward the ceiling, taking the shape of a woman dressed in a flowing white gown. The woman's skin was bloodless and white, and her eyes were drained of all color. She was the Yuki-onna. The snow demon.

Hovering above the two men, the ice demon watched them both, her pale lips turned up in a cruel smile. There was much blood here. Warm blood, still pulsing through the veins of mortals. Pangs of hunger filled her. It had been too long since she had tasted blood. Her hunger must be appeased.

Her pale eyes were drawn at last to the cut on Mosaku's forehead. She smiled again, baring the tips of sharp, white teeth as she drifted down. Her arms enveloped Mosaku like suffocating wings, and her lips touched his throat. Mosaku stirred once, and then he never moved again.

Chapter Five

Cleo rode her elevator up to the second floor with a pile of books and a bowl of tahini chicken in her lap. She always had mixed feelings about conversations with her mother. On the one hand, she loved it that her mother worried so much about her and Alex. They *were* acting strange, so it made sense. On the other hand, Cleo wished her mom would stop paying so much attention to them so they could concentrate on finding their father. Their mother would never believe their stories about traveling to a mythical world, and even if she did, what good would it do? The last thing she needed was more to worry about.

Their mother was better off thinking that Alex was having girl troubles. Cleo chuckled to herself. *Girl troubles.* As though any girl would be attracted to a dork like Alex.

As she thought this, Cleo wheeled herself into the den and powered up the plasma screen . . .

. . . just in time to see the terrifyingly beautiful woman hovering over her brother and the old woodcutter.

"Oh my God," Cleo whispered, her voice small with fright. She could only stare in horror as the ghostly figure settled over the old Japanese man and pressed her face against his neck. For a moment Cleo had no idea what the woman was doing . . . until the pale figure raised herself up and Cleo saw the blood dripping from her fangs.

The old woodcutter's body was as pale as snow. Floating in the air, the ice demon drifted toward Alex.

"Alex!" Cleo yelled into the computer mike. "Wake up!"

Alex didn't stir. "Listen to me!" Cleo yelled. "Wake up!"

The young man's eyes flickered open and he looked about dreamily.

"Wake up *now*!" Cleo screamed.

Alex sat up and took in everything at once. He saw Mosaku, pale as death. He saw the ice demon floating in the air. And he saw the blood dripping from her fangs.

That was enough to shock Alex into wakefulness. He sat upright and scrambled backward, away from the wraithlike figure.

"Get out of there!" Cleo screamed.

Alex got to his knees and crawled toward the door. The Yuki-onna raised herself up, then let out a breath of icy air so cold, it could be seen like a frosty mist. Her breath touched Alex, freezing him in his tracks. Every muscle in his body locked up as though trapped in ice, and he fell back to the floor.

The Yuki-onna drifted over him, hovering just a few inches from his face. Her features were beautiful but cold and hard. She reached out to touch him like a cat playing with a mouse. The ends of her fingers were tipped with wicked claws. A smile played across her lips, which were still tinged red with Mosaku's blood. Her colorless eyes settled on Alex's, and the smile faded a little. She seemed suddenly less sure of herself, and more interested, as though the cat had decided that the mouse was more than just a plaything.

"Tell me your name," she said in a voice as hollow and soulless as the wind.

Alex could hardly speak. He barely remembered the name he was supposed to use in the Alterworld. "Al— Minokichi. My name's Minokichi."

One of her razorlike claws traced a line along his cheek. "You're a beautiful boy, Minokichi."

"Thanks," Alex said. "I guess."

The Yuki-onna hesitated a moment, struggling with some sort of decision. Finally, she whispered, "Consider yourself fortunate, Minokichi. For tonight, I spare your life. Never before have I denied myself the warmth of a human's blood."

"Th-thank you," he stammered.

"Mmm, but your life comes with a price." The ice demon lowered herself until they were almost touching. Her eyes locked onto his, staring deeply into him. He couldn't look away. He felt imprisoned by her gaze.

"Swear you will not tell a soul what you saw tonight."

Unable to speak, Alex only nodded.

"Swear it! Say the words!"

Alex struggled to make his muscles work. "I . . . I swear!" he gasped at last.

She smiled a ghastly smile. "I'll know if you break your promise," she said. "Understand that."

Terrified, Alex nodded again.

The Yuki-onna gave another terrifying smile, touching him tenderly once more with the sharp tip of her claw. Slowly, she rose up into the air until she was almost at the hut's ceiling. Her female figure vanished, to be replaced by a thick white fog that swirled as though blown by the north wind. Then the mist flowed out the door, and the ice demon was gone.

Chapter Six

Through the monitor, Cleo watched as Alex lay motionless.

"Alex? Are you okay?"

At first he didn't respond. The ice demon's grip relaxed only slowly, and it took a while before he could move. Finally, Alex sat up. "Yeah, I think so."

"Alex, check him. Quick."

Alex felt as if his arms and legs were made of lead, but he managed to drag himself over to Mosaku. The old woodcutter's skin was pale and cold. There was no life in him. Every drop of blood had been drained from his body.

"Yuki-onna," he whispered.

"What?" Cleo asked.

Alex explained. "Yuki-onna. The snow demon. He told me about her. About what she does to people." He looked up into the air. "Where were you?"

"I was with Mom. Sorry."

Alex looked down at Mosaku again. He felt crushed. He'd only known the old man for a short time, but the woodcutter had been charming and full of life. In the brief moments they'd spent together, Mosaku had reminded Alex of his own father, who was both friend and mentor. Alex told himself that none of this was real, but it didn't do any good. When he was in the Alterworld, everything he touched and every person he met was as real as anyone back home.

He heaved a sigh, trying to push past his sorrow. He was here for a reason: to find his father. "Well, at least we figured out what this myth is about. Have you ever heard of this Yuki-onna?"

Cleo's voice replied, "Never. I'll look it up, though. There can't be that many Japanese snow demons." She paused. "Hey, is it my imagination, or is something changing? The hut looks and sounds different."

Alex looked around and realized that Cleo was right. Watching through the monitor, she noticed backgrounds and scenes better than he could. Turning, he saw more light gleaming through cracks in the hut's door. The cold was gone, and what was more, the sound of winter wind had been replaced by . . . birdsong.

Rising to his feet, Alex threw open the door. Bright sunlight streamed in, and a blue sky spread above him. Nearby, the happy sound of running water rose from a river that had been frozen solid an hour ago, and birds sang in leaf-covered trees.

Alex's jaw dropped. "I've heard of short winters, but this is ridiculous. What's going on?"

Cleo considered what was happening. Everything they saw was new ground for them—from the myths themselves to actually being inside the Alterworld—so she didn't have much to go on. But she guessed that if the Gorgos Stone was somehow making the myths become real, then the Alterworld would follow the story as it had been passed down. "This myth must take place over a long period of time," she said at last. "Whatever's waiting for you outside that door must connect to the ice vampire somehow."

"Any ice vampire that's waiting out there is probably a puddle already. Geez, it's hot. I'm taking off this coat." He stripped away the coat but hesitated to go outside. "This is weird. What happened to the time? What happens to me when it changes? Do I grow older too?"

"Maybe," Cleo guessed, "if that's part of the myth."

"Well, here goes nothing."

Alex stepped out of the ferryman's hut. Instantly, the Alterworld flowed around him, then readjusted. It was sort of like entering the Alterworld itself—but not quite so disorienting. The whole world seemed to shift slightly, and suddenly Alex found himself standing before a large tree, holding an ax that he had just sunk into the trunk. He hefted the ax. "I wonder how you say *Paul Bunyan* in Japanese." He looked around. He guessed he was in the same forest as before.

"So where do I go from here?" he asked Cleo. "I'm sure not going to get any closer to Dad standing around here chopping wood."

"This myth is moving through time," Cleo theorized. "Maybe you just have to let it carry you along and see where it takes you."

"Ooh," Alex said, "I think this myth just took a turn for the better."

A figure had appeared, walking through the trees. It was a Japanese girl with beautiful black hair and bright black eyes. In one hand she carried a red-and-white bird in a wooden cage. In the other hand she held a wooden stand that matched the cage, except that it was broken.

"Hello," the young woman said with a smile that was even more beautiful than her eyes.

"Hi yourself," Alex said with a grin.

"I think I might be lost," the girl said timidly. "I've never walked in this part of the forest before."

Alex nodded, trying to think of something witty to say. "It's, um, a big forest. It's easy to get lost if you're not with someone who knows their way around."

Cleo's bemused voice sounded in his ear. "Alex, are you flirting with her?"

"Buzz off," he whispered.

The girl looked at the trees, which were covered with bright red bark.

"What kind of trees are these?" she asked.

"Oh, they're called Blood Trees," Alex said, as though it were common knowledge. "They call them that because—" He was about to say, "because of the Yuki-onna," but then he remembered his promise to the snow demon. The girl was looking at him expectantly, so he said lamely, "—because the trees are so red."

An awkward pause followed. It was the kind of awkward pause Alex was used to experiencing whenever he tried to impress a girl. But this girl was different. She didn't laugh at him or roll her eyes. She smiled at him politely, so he said, "Maybe I can help. What are you looking for?"

The girl replied, "A woodcutter named Minokichi. They told me he'd be working in the forest today."

"This is your lucky day, then," he said.

"You're Minokichi?" She looked pleased.

He laughed. "I have been all day."

"My name is Yuki." The beautiful girl bowed. Her hair tumbled like black silk down her shoulders. "They told me there was nobody better at fixing anything made of wood than you."

Alex put down his ax and puffed out his chest.

He knew absolutely nothing about woodworking, but then he wasn't himself—he was Minokichi. And Minokichi was, apparently, an expert. "That's what they say. What can I do for you?"

Yuki held up her cage and stand. "My cage is broken. I'm afraid my bird will fly away."

Alex took the cage from her carefully. As he did, his fingers brushed hers and he felt her tremble. Her eyes dropped down to her feet, and she blushed.

Alex made a show of examining the cage, though really he was looking through its slim wooden bars at Yuki's face. After a moment, he said, "I'd be glad to fix it for you. . . . It would give me an excuse to see you again."

Yuki looked up and smiled a smile that made his heart race. It occurred to him that maybe he was *supposed* to find her attractive—maybe that was part of the myth of Minokichi. Maybe the myth was influencing the way he thought and felt. *Maybe,* he thought, *but then again, I don't think I care.*

"If you bring it to my house, I'll give you tea," she offered.

He smiled. "I'll have it to you by the end of the day."

Yuki bowed again and turned to leave. Then, hesitating, she turned back and giggled. "They told me you were a great woodworker, Minokichi. But they didn't tell me you were so handsome."

With another laugh, she hurried away through the woods, leaving Alex blushing and happy, the blood singing in his veins. He watched until she was lost behind the trees and Cleo interrupted his daydream.

"Okay, what the heck just happened? I felt like I was watching a very bad soap opera."

"All soap operas are bad," he shot back.

"Not nearly as bad as that little episode. Whatever happened to 'I've got to find Dad'?"

Alex snapped out of his trance and threw an annoying gaze out to Cleo, wherever she was. "Chill out, Clo. You were the one who said things in these myths happen for a reason. I'm just taking your suggestion and going with the flow."

"Yeah, well, you just keep that flow heading toward the end of the myth and don't get sidetracked."

Instead of responding, Alex sat down on a tree stump and began to examine the birdcage.

He'd hardly even looked at a birdcage before, let alone tried to fix one.

His fingers flew over the cage, finding hinges, ties, everything that held the wooden structure together. He thought he might—or, rather, Minokichi might—be able to fix it after all. Then he could visit Yuki.

In the Bellowses' study, Cleo watched her brother fiddle with the wooden sticks. She'd never seen him get so involved in a myth before. Usually, he wanted nothing more than to get out as soon as possible. Now he seemed to be fully involved in the myth, even to be enjoying it.

"Um, Alex, do you have a minute to concentrate on the business at hand?"

"Sure, shoot," he said absently, still studying the birdcage.

She sighed, her patience wearing thin. "I wasn't able to turn up anything in Dad's reference material about the Gorgos Stone. I'm thinking of paying a visit to Max Asher."

That got Alex's attention. He put the cage down and rubbed his chin thoughtfully. "Cleo, hold it. Think about this a minute. We can't risk bringing anyone else into this."

"And we can't risk fumbling around in the dark anymore either. I won't tell him what we're doing. I don't think he'd believe me anyway. I just want to find out what he knows about the stone."

She could see Alex considering her suggestion. Finally, he looked up and out into the air. "Okay, your call, sis. If you need me, you know where to find me."

Cleo frowned. "At Yuki's?"

Alex grinned. "You bet."

Cleo groaned and pushed herself away from the computer console. There was trouble ahead. Normally when Alex was inside a myth, she feared for his life and limb. This time, she feared for his heart.

Chapter Seven

"Well, well, two Bellows women in one day!"

Max Asher stood at the door of his tidy house, one hand holding a book and the other on the doorknob. He seemed genuinely happy to see Cleo, and he stepped aside instantly, giving her room to wheel her chair into his house. He motioned her toward a couch and sat down as she steadied her chair near him.

"It's been a long time since you've been for a visit, my dear," Max said.

Cleo nodded, happy to be making small

talk. She wasn't exactly sure how she was going to phrase her request, so the chitchat made everything easier.

"You're not home all that often, from what my dad tells me."

The old man chuckled and set his book aside. "Well, it's true, it's true. Lecturing here, doing research there. I am away quite a bit." He smiled at her. "Well, dear Cleo, to what do I owe this honor?"

Cleo bit her lip. She'd rehearsed her opening lines several times on the way over, but nothing sounded right. So she settled on the direct approach. "Mom said you visited her today. She said you told her about a stone that might have something to do with what happened to Dad."

Max blinked, as though waiting for Cleo to add something. When she said nothing, he prompted her. "Yes . . . and did she tell you anything more? The name of the stone, perhaps?"

"No, not really. I just . . . I was just surprised. You know, everyone else thinks Dad just ran off with some treasure—"

"But you don't think so," the old professor said. "Perhaps you know something about it?"

"Wh—? No! No," she stammered. "I just want to know more about it. In case Alex and I happen to come across it."

Note to self, she thought. *I am a lousy liar.*

Max raised an eyebrow. "In case you come across it?"

"Yes," Cleo replied. "Alex and I go through Dad's books. There's a chance we might find something about the stone in them."

Max reached out and patted Cleo on the shoulder. "If you did come across it, you'd do well to tell your mother or me immediately."

Cleo continued to play dumb. "So, what, it's dangerous?"

"That's a good question. The Gorgos Stone is something that everyone in archaeology has heard rumors of but nobody knows much about." He stood up and walked toward the window, pacing as though giving a lecture at the university. "If you believe some of the stories, Gorgos was a trickster god."

"Like Loki in Norse mythology," Cleo said, remembering a previous adventure she and Alex had gone through. "A troublemaker."

"Similar," Max agreed. "But as the story goes, he had no myth of his own and lived to corrupt the myths of the other gods. The rest of the gods banded together and somehow trapped him in that stone. According to the legend, the stone was hidden away so that no one would ever be able to release him."

Cleo felt a sense of dread creep up her spine and into her neck, like the cold fingers of the ice demon. "And what if someone did find the stone? And if they found a way to release Gorgos?"

Max looked at her, his gaze sharp and penetrating, as though she were a mystery he was trying to unravel. "We're talking hypothetically now, yes?"

Cleo swallowed. "Well, of course."

"Hypothetically, then, the unspeakably evil Gorgos would be unleashed on the world again."

The cold fingers gripped Cleo and she nearly gasped. "It's . . . it's just a myth, though, right?"

Max shrugged. "I'll tell you, Cleo, that I don't know what it means to say something is 'just a myth.' Myths make up the center of our entire culture. They make up the heart of every culture, whether it is primitive or modern. Everything we do, everything we think is influenced by myths in some way."

"How is that possible?" Cleo asked. "I

mean, how could some old stories about gods that no one believes in affect us?"

Max chuckled. "Sometimes it's the gods you don't believe in that can cause the most trouble. But seriously, Cleo, you must stop thinking of myths as being so ancient and out of date. The deep myths are still with us. Let me give you just one example. What would it mean to you if I told you I could make you a star?"

The teen looked for some secret answer. Finding none, she settled for the obvious. "You'd make me famous. A celebrity."

"Exactly," the professor replied. "Famous. Like ancient heroes and villains were famous. Do you know what happened to the great heroes of ancient Greece?" Cleo shook her head. "The gods scooped them up and put them in the heavens. Sometimes it was a reward, and sometimes it was a punishment. But it was always permanent. Back then, famous people were quite literally—"

"—made into stars," Cleo concluded. "That's where the expression comes from."

"Well, that's one place it comes from," Max said. "And if all the ancient myths were rewritten, it would alter something that we do today. Perhaps the resulting change would be small, but perhaps," he said, his tone turning very serious, "perhaps it would change the world.

"Besides," Max continued, "new myths are being created all the time. The stories become part of the fabric that binds us all together." He clasped his hands together, intertwining his fingers. "And if that fabric is torn, well—" He pulled his fingers apart violently.

Seeing the frightened look on Cleo's face, Max put an arm around her shoulder. "Don't worry, Cleo. I'm far more concerned with human threats. If the stone really does exist, there are people who'd do anything to get their hands on it. I've been careful in my inquiries about it the last few days. I don't want a raft of treasure hunters crawling all over your family."

"Of course," Cleo said in a weak voice.

"Cleo," Max said hesitantly, "why do I get the feeling that you're not telling me everything you know?"

"I don't know," she responded quickly. "I'm just worried about Dad, I guess."

Max sighed. "We all are, Cleo. We all are."

Chapter Eight

The forest that in winter had been so cold and threatening was now alive with the promise of life. Birds sang in the trees or flitted through the air. Shafts of sunlight fell to the earth like golden columns that held the sky aloft. The river seemed to flow more noisily than before, laughing as it ran down to some ocean far away.

Once he'd fixed the birdcage, Alex had started walking, and his feet had naturally found a path through the woods. He let the path carry him forward, and soon he found himself strolling toward a small cottage with rice-paper walls and a slanted roof. Nervously, he straightened his robes and smoothed back his hair. Then he walked up to the cottage porch and knocked on the door.

A moment later the door opened, and Yuki stood there beaming. She looked even more beautiful than she had before.

"You fixed it!" she said in delight, looking down at the birdcage.

"As promised," Alex said proudly.

"Please, come in."

Alex followed her into the cottage. It was small but very neat. In ancient Japan there was no glass in the windows, of course, but they were covered with rice-paper curtains so thin that they let in a great deal of sunlight. The soft light that gathered in the room made Alex feel relaxed.

A low table sat in the middle of the room. It had already been set with a beautiful arrangement of orange and yellow flowers, and beside the flowers sat a teapot, two clay bowls, and two cups. Yuki motioned for Alex to sit; then she took a place across from him. Without saying a word, she poured powdered green tea into a bowl, then added boiling water from the kettle.

Steam rose up, filling the room with a fresh, rich scent. Yuki took up a small bamboo brush and began to whisk the tea vigorously.

"This is a lot of work to go through for a cup of tea. Back where I come from, we'd just throw in a bag or two."

Yuki carefully placed the bamboo brush back on the tray. "The tea ceremony is an art form. Through one's interpretation of the age-old ritual, one expresses something inside." She looked down modestly. "Or something one feels for someone else."

Delicately, the girl lifted one cup of tea and held it out to Alex. He took it gratefully. His hand brushed against hers, and this time it was no accident.

"What are you expressing, Yuki?" he asked softly.

"My joy at having you here with me."

Alex felt his face tingle with a blush, but he forced himself not to turn away. He wanted to see her face, and he wanted her to see the emotions her words drew out of him. She bore his gaze for a moment, then turned her dark eyes toward the floor.

"Why are you alone here?" Alex asked.

Yuki looked around the cottage. She seemed

to be doing anything to keep from staring into his eyes. "My parents died. The winters are hard here in the forest. I've been alone . . . for a very long time."

Alex cleared his throat. "How about guys? I'd think they'd be all over you. Why aren't you seeing anyone?"

Yuki looked confused for a moment. "You mean suitors. I've never had a suitor. I never felt the need . . . before."

They drank their tea in silence as Alex tried to absorb the meaning of her words along with the hot steam of the tea. He sipped the tea and felt it trickle down his throat. This moment felt right to him somehow. He was sure he belonged here, at this moment. He wanted it to last.

When they had both finished their tea, Yuki stood up and carried the cups to a small kitchen washbasin. Alex followed her.

"Let me help you."

He took the cups from her and put them in a small tub of water near the hearth.

"And what about you?" Yuki asked. "There is no special girl in your life?"

Her question made Alex think about his own life as much as Minokichi's. He said, "Well, I guess the way things have worked out lately . . .

you know, family stuff and everything . . . I've been too busy to think about girls."

He looked at her, and this time she did not look away. Her eyes were jet-black and deep, with, Alex could tell, many thoughts behind them. He felt himself getting lost in them, and he pulled back long enough to say, "You said before that you've never needed a suitor. You think you might ever change your mind?"

The corners of her mouth turned up into a small, sweet smile. "I haven't known you long, Minokichi—but the truth is, I think I might have already found one."

Alex opened his arms and Yuki fell into them. To Alex, that moment felt as right as any moment in his entire life. His arms seemed made to hold just this girl in just this way, and he sighed deeply as Yuki settled into his embrace.

But if Cleo had been watching on the monitor, she would have seen what Alex could not. As he and Yuki embraced, a cold wind blew through the cottage. With her head on his shoulder, Yuki raised her face toward the ceiling, and as she did, her eyes turned clear and ghostly while her face paled and grew angry. Then, as she gave a shake of her head, Yuki's eyes regained their jet-black depth and she buried her head in Alex's neck.

Chapter Nine

Cleo returned from Max Asher's house more unsettled than when she'd left. She'd hoped her father's old friend would tell her something that would make her feel better, but instead he'd only reminded her of how dangerous and mysterious the whole affair was. In one sense, Max was right—the human element was dangerous. It was possible that some person had been after the stone, and that person might be responsible for her father's disappearance.

Another possibility was equally frightening— that the Gorgos Stone was real and possessed real power. The very idea would have sounded ridiculous to Cleo only a short time ago. But she and her brother had experienced strange events firsthand. During his trip to the myth of the Norse god Loki, Alex had tried to tamper with the myth. In doing so, he had nearly set off a catastrophic earthquake in the real world. Could the Gorgos Stone have been responsible for that? If so, what might it do in the hands of someone who really wanted to cause trouble?

Fortunately, Cleo's mother had returned to her work in the kitchen, so she hardly noticed when Cleo rolled by and went up the elevator. Cleo wheeled into the study and was surprised by what she saw on the plasma screen. Alex was sleeping in a cottage she had never seen before. It looked warm and cozy, with a small kitchen off to one side and a carefully crafted table made of black wood sitting in the middle. Alex was lying, very still, on a small mat.

"Alex, wake up!"

"What?" Alex nearly jumped out of his robe, startled by her voice in his ear. He looked around, bleary-eyed, trying to make sense of his surroundings. "What's going on?"

"Alex, are you all right?"

Her brother rubbed his eyes and shook himself, trying to shrug both sleep and sudden fear from his shoulders. "All right, of course I'm all right. What's up with you, Cleo?"

Cleo was annoyed. "What's up with *me*? What are *you* doing? I thought the ice vampire had gotten to you."

Alex touched his own skin, feeling its warmth, and chuckled. "I guess not. Where's Yuki? She was just here."

He stood and looked out a window that was now open. Outside he saw another beautiful spring day unfolding—but he had a sense that it was not the same spring day as before.

"Man, how long have I been asleep?" He yawned. "Oh, never mind that. How did it go with Max?"

Cleo furrowed her brow in concern. "I'm not sure. He told me about Gorgos and the stone. He said that Gorgos was some kind of trickster and the gods imprisoned him in the stone."

Alex guessed the rest. "And what, Dad let him out?"

"I don't know. Not into our world, but somehow maybe he got out into the Cyber-Museum."

"And what about the stone?" Alex looked around, distracted. He wondered where Yuki had gone.

"Don't know that, either," Cleo admitted. "Maybe it's in there. Maybe Dad didn't know what it was and tried to scan it into the computer. Whatever, it's still our best starting place to look for Dad." She paused. "And speaking of looking for Dad, what are you doing sleeping in some strange cottage?"

"What do you mean? I don't know why I fell asleep, but this is Yuki's place. I—"

Alex looked around again. For the first time, he realized that the cottage looked different. It was still Yuki's—he recognized the tea set in the corner and the washbasin in the kitchen—but it also looked different. Less lonely, more lived in. "It's Yuki's . . . I think. It looks different. And I don't remember falling asleep. I think the myth must be moving again."

"Be careful, Alex. If she's moving with it, she must be part of the story."

Alex was immediately alarmed. "You mean she could be the snow demon's next victim?"

"Maybe. Or maybe you are."

The door flew open and Yuki walked in,

carrying a full, sloshing bucket of water. She put the bucket down next to the washbasin and kissed Alex on the cheek. A lock of her hair fell forward, brushing Alex's skin.

"Good morning, husband. I thought you'd never wake today."

"Husband?" Cleo screeched.

Chapter Ten

Alex's jaw nearly hit the floor. A short time ago they were strangers. Now suddenly they were husband and wife? *If we really are married,* he thought, *the Japanese take those tea ceremonies more seriously than I thought!*

"So, um, we're actually . . . married?" he asked.

Now it was Yuki's turn to be confused. Seeing her bewildered look, Alex tried to cover. "Uh, I mean, of course we're married. I just find it hard to believe sometimes." He gathered her into a comforting hug. "I've been so happy."

Yuki put her head on his shoulder. "So have I. I never thought I'd feel what I feel for you, Minokichi."

She kissed him on the nose and pulled away mischievously. "But there's time enough to talk later. Right now, there's a forest full of trees waiting for you, and a thousand and one chores I must take care of."

Yuki turned away from him and started arranging her long hair. She swept it into a bun atop her head and secured it with a graceful comb. Every move she made was delicate and precise. Then, once she was properly coiffed, she gathered up some gardening tools. Before she got to the door, Alex called out, "Yuki."

The girl—now more like a woman—turned and looked at him, the innocent smile still on her face.

Alex stammered, "Be—be careful out there."

Yuki laughed. "Why?"

Alex worked his jaw, tempted to warn her about the snow demon. But he had made a promise. He had no idea what would happen if he broke it, but considering what the monster had done to Mosaku, he didn't want to find out. Finally, he just said, "It's . . . it's dangerous in the woods. I don't know what I'd do if you were hurt."

Yuki laughed again, brushing his worries aside. "I can take care of myself, husband. Maybe it's the woods that should look out."

With another breezy laugh, she hurried outside.

Alex's smile chased her out the door. Perfect. She was perfect. No wonder he—or, rather, Minokichi—had married her. She was demure, confident, and quick-witted. Every man in the village must have been in love with her.

Cleo spoke over the monitor. "You didn't tell her about the snow demon."

Alex shook his head. "I can't. The demon said she'd know if I told someone. I . . . I couldn't take that chance."

From the monitor, Cleo watched Alex's face. He stared longingly at the door, as though trying to see Yuki through the walls.

"Alex," she said. "You've got to start thinking more about finding Dad and less about romance."

"Yeah, yeah, I'm on it," he said, shaking himself out of his reverie. He walked across the cottage to the washbasin and splashed cold water on his face. As he straightened up and dabbed his face with a towel, he caught sight of himself in a mirror. It was the same face he'd seen before, but it looked a little more worn.

The wind suddenly howled, banging against the door. Cold air found a crack in the wall and slipped inside, running up Alex's back and freezing his spine. He shivered. He hurried to the door and opened it. Outside, the world had turned to winter once again. No snow was falling, but the sky was heavy and gray, and the wind had already stripped the trees of their leaves.

"The only way to go is forward, right?" he said, trying to brace himself.

"Seems that way," Cleo replied.

Not knowing what else to do, Alex followed the hint left by Yuki. He saw his ax leaning against the wall. He picked it up and rested it on his shoulder, then stepped out into the cool winter air. So far, each time shift had led to something new, so he assumed it would happen again this time. He figured he would just keep walking until it did.

He heard a shuffling through the leaves covering the forest floor, but when he looked he saw nothing. Then he heard it again, but still no one was out there.

"Clo, did you see anything?"

"No," she said. "What's up?"

Something kicked up snow to his right. This time he thought he saw a flash of something squat and brown scurrying between two trees. Alex stopped walking, and the sounds stopped too.

"I don't know, Clo. I've got the distinct feeling I'm being stalked."

Clop-clop!

"I heard it too," Cleo said.

Alex fingered the ax on his shoulder. "Aren't there any myths about rabbits or baby seals? In Tahiti? Rabbits and baby seals in Tahiti. Now, that would make me more comfortable."

Suddenly, a gnarled figure jumped out from behind a tree. Its back was bent, and strands of long, thin gray hair hung from its head. The figure's face was wrinkled and its eyes bulged. Startled, Alex stepped back, his white knuckles clutching the handle of his ax.

"Minokichi!" the figure screeched.

Alex took another step back. "Yes . . ."

"You don't remember me?" The figure laughed grimly and stepped closer. It was a woman, a very old woman, bent with age. "Noriko, Mosaku's wife. His widow."

Alex barely recognized her. The cheery older woman he'd seen earlier was gone, replaced by this gnarled hag. It wasn't just that she had grown old—something else had changed her. She wore misery about her like a thin blanket against the coming cold.

"Oh, yeah, sorry. It's been a long time."

Noriko nodded, her bulging eyes studying him. "It has. Life has been hard for me since my husband was taken. But for you things seem sweet."

Alex looked down at his own clothes. Clean, comfortable, new. "I, um, I guess so." Her wild-eyed stare made him uncomfortable. "Well, it was good seeing you."

He started to walk past her, but she stepped in front of him, pointing one wrinkled finger at his chest. "Walk on, Minokichi. But realize that what happened to my husband could happen to you . . . or to your children."

Alex was shocked. "I . . . I've got kids?"

Noriko ignored his surprise. In the myth, Minokichi obviously knew of his children, so the question didn't make sense to her. She thought he was toying with her. The old woman clutched his arm desperately. "Listen to me, Minokichi.

Your wife is not what she seems. Don't turn your back on her."

The mention of Yuki's name roused Alex's anger. "Lady, let go of me." He pulled his arm roughly from her grip and stepped away from her. "Look, I'm sorry about what happened to Mosaku, but you can't blame that on Yuki!" The anger drained away quickly—he could feel nothing but pity for this old woman, trembling in the cold, miserable at the loss of her husband. "Look, what happened to Mosaku was horrible. It could make anyone a little unbalanced. . . ."

"You think I'm crazy," the old woman moaned.

"With grief," Alex explained. "It could happen to anyone."

The old woman laughed again, a joyless laugh as sharp and bitter as the wind. "Maybe I am crazy. But that doesn't change what I know. Be careful when the snow comes again, Minokichi."

There was nothing Alex could do or say for Noriko, so he just stepped past her and kept walking. He could feel her wild eyes on his back. As he hurried to put distance between them, he heard her shout, "Listen to me! Be careful when the snow comes!"

Alex refused to look back. He felt pity for Noriko, and suddenly he felt guilt, too. He had slept through Mosaku's death. . . . He had survived when others had not. Now Noriko lived in misery and madness, and he—or, rather, Minokichi—was leading a happy life with a wife and children. It didn't seem right.

"What was that about?" Cleo's voice reached him through the computer.

"I don't know," Alex said, hurrying along. "But this myth seems to be moving faster. I don't think I had any kids this morning."

Chapter Eleven

In the Bellows house, Cleo sat at the desk with the computer on one side and an old book of Japanese myths open before her. She thumbed through the pages with a growing sense of urgency. When Alex was inside a myth he risked real danger. Cleo feared it was only a matter of time before the snow demon tried to claim its next victim.

Cleo turned a page and found an illustration of the Yuki-onna, pictured as a beautiful and terrible female demon. In the drawing beside the demon stood a frightened young

Japanese man who could only be Minokichi. There was a page full of writing, but it was all in Japanese ideograms.

"Alex," she explained, leaning toward the microphone, "I've found this story in a Japanese myth book, but I need to get it translated."

"Translated?" Alex asked, still walking aimlessly among the winter trees. "How?"

"By someone who can read Japanese," she replied.

"No kidding," he groaned. "But who? What are you going to tell them? You can't just bring someone else into this—"

"Hold your ax there, fella. They don't have to know what I'm doing. I'll just be asking a question for a school project. We have to find out what's going on in this myth, and fast."

Cleo continued, "I'm going to visit Max Asher again. He'll know something about this myth. Oh, and Alex?" she added, trying to fend off her worry with a light tone.

"Yeah?"

"Try not to have any more kids while I'm gone, okay?"

He heard her laughing as she rolled away from the computer.

• • •

Very funny, he thought. *A thousand laughs.* Let *her* get stuck inside a myth with an ice demon creeping up, and then see how funny she thought it was. *Sisters.*

Alex stepped onto a path he thought he recognized and followed it to his cottage. The pleasant smells of cooking food drifted toward him, and he quickened his pace, jumping onto the porch and pushing open the door. Instantly two young children—a boy and a girl—leaped to their feet and ran toward him.

"Daddy!" They nearly tackled him. Alex laughed, startled and amused, and fell onto his back with the children on top of him. Obviously, these were his children. But he wasn't really a father. What was he supposed to do? Not knowing how else to act, he remembered things his father used to do with him when he was small. He grabbed the little boy and picked him up, holding him in the air and then lowering him for a kiss on the forehead. Then he rolled over and picked up the girl, grabbing her hands and spinning her around. They were about three and five years old, big enough and heavy enough to tire him out after only a few swings.

"More! More!" they shouted, laughing.

Yuki, who sat beside the cooking fire, looked up with a smile. "No, children, it's late."

"That's right," Alex said, giving them each a pat. "Time for you guys to get into bed."

The two children groaned and complained—something Alex recalled vividly from his own childhood—but eventually they relented and scurried toward a back room, divided from the main living area by a rice-paper screen. Alex heard them arguing and went back to break up a little skirmish and remind them to go to sleep. He returned to the main part of the house and slumped to the floor beside the small black table in the center of the room.

He sighed. "I never knew being a parent was such hard work. Man, when I think of what I put my mom and dad through . . ."

Yuki kissed him on the cheek. "I'm sure you were a good son."

Alex put his arm around her and held her close, his heart racing. "I was hoping we'd get some time alone."

Yuki put her forehead against his. "I think that can be arranged."

She kissed him on the nose—the second time she'd done that. It was sweet and affectionate, a small ritual he sensed they had enacted thousands of times over the years, reminding each other of their love. When Yuki kissed him like that, he genuinely *felt* something for her. Was it love? Could he fall in love in the Alterworld? The people in myths didn't just seem real—they *were* real. As real as anyone he'd ever met in the real world. And Yuki obviously loved Minokichi. They had spent years together, started a family together, and even now she doted on him.

He watched her work on their dinner, stirring the pot of soup with her back to him. And even though this was the Alterworld and the myth was flowing by at high speed, he still knew he had enjoyed these moments night after night for a long time. It felt comfortable to him. Sitting there watching Yuki reminded him of all the little gestures his mother and father shared, small comforts created over their years together.

The thought of his father hit Alex like a slap in the face. His father—that was the reason he was in the Alterworld in the first place. He had to uncover the connections among the Japanese symbols, the Gorgos Stone, and his father. And that meant understanding this myth.

"I, um, I met a woman today," he said.

"A woman?" Yuki asked over her shoulder. "Which woman?"

"Noriko. She was Mosaku's wife."

Yuki stopped stirring. "Oh?"

"I think his death made her a little crazy."

Yuki nodded, still with her back to him. "I can imagine."

"She said I was in danger." He glanced toward the screen behind which the children had gone to bed. "And the kids."

Now Yuki turned around. She stared at him, her face still soft but her jaw set and her eyes flashing. "Really. And what are you in danger from?"

Alex looked down, unable to meet her gaze. "She said . . . she said from you."

At the sound of those words, Yuki turned on Alex, her eyes flashing, and flew into a rage.

Chapter Twelve

"How dare she! How dare she!" Yuki shouted. Alex stepped back, surprised by her reaction. He wasn't sure what he'd been expecting, but it wasn't this sudden flood of emotion. Yuki looked as if she was about to burst into tears and explode with rage at the same time. She waved her spoon around like a weapon. "She's a crazy old woman and she shouldn't be allowed to run around scaring people."

The dam burst, and tears poured from Yuki's eyes. Instinctively, Alex reached out and pulled her close. "Yuki. Yuki," he whispered, trying to soothe her. "Easy . . . I didn't say I believed her. I just told you because I thought it was strange."

Yuki sniffed, trying to recover her composure. "People should be more careful what they say to each other, husband." She wiped tears from her eyes and heaved one deep, calming sigh. "I just don't want anything to ever come between us."

Alex smiled and brushed a stray hair back behind her ear. "Don't worry. Nothing will come between us."

Yuki hugged him close, leaning her head against his shoulder. He could not see her eyes turn cold and pale as snow. "Yes," she said. "I am sure you are right."

Cold. Darkness. That was all Noriko ever felt these days, and all she ever saw. Warmth and light had been stolen from her the day her husband died. Most thought poor Mosaku had simply spent one too many days out in the snow—working too hard, taking too many risks to gather wood for his work. They said Minokichi was lucky not to have been lost with him. Minokichi himself had been silent on the subject, claiming he had simply awakened to find Mosaku frozen on the ground.

Noriko knew better. She knew her husband was too crafty to fall victim to a little winter blizzard. He had been as tough as a tree, that old man. It would have taken a far greater power to bring him down.

It would have taken the Yuki-onna.

Noriko knew. She saw it in Minokichi's eyes. Something haunted him, something he refused to tell. It was a secret the woodcutter had kept hidden for years, a secret that was now hidden behind the protective walls of his marriage and family. But she would tear down those walls. She would find that secret.

The darkness and cold did not stop Noriko that evening. She trudged through the chilly night, determined to reach Minokichi's house and confront him again. And if the woman was there, so much the better. Noriko would make Minokichi admit the truth about what had happened to Mosaku.

Cold.

It breathed down Noriko's back, freezing, as though an entire winter had gathered on her shoulders. The old woman shuddered and spun around. Nothing. No one. Just the darkness and the cold.

Noriko turned to continue along the path and screamed.

The Yuki-onna was there, floating in the air before her face. The ice demon was as pale as snow, wrapped in flowing white robes. Her colorless eyes glared at Noriko, and she smiled, showing sharp teeth.

"Where is *your* husband, Noriko?" the Yuki-onna purred.

The old woman screamed again. She turned once more to run the other way, but somehow the ice demon was there before her. The Yuki-onna spread her arms wide. "Would you like to join him?"

"No," Noriko whispered in terror. "No, please . . ."

She turned and ran blindly. For a moment she thought she'd gotten away. The ice demon was nowhere in sight. Noriko sprinted ahead, stumbling and falling, regaining her feet, and running some more. Her hands and knees were cut, but she ignored the pain. She kept running . . .

. . . until she felt freezing hands clamp around her neck, and a deep, sharp pain, as though her bones had turned to ice.

Chapter Thirteen

A shiver ran through Cleo. She didn't know why, since Max Asher's house was warm and pleasant. But something made her shiver anyway.

Probably nerves, she thought. *Get ahold of yourself. You have to make this work.*

"What is it you wanted again?" Max Asher was asking.

Cleo smoothed her skirt over her legs, mostly as an excuse to keep from looking this family friend in the eye. "To translate an old Japanese story."

Max eyed her suspiciously. She knew what he

was thinking—she'd hardly ever spoken to him before, and now she was asking him for information twice in one day. "This project wouldn't have anything to do with the Gorgos Stone, would it?"

"What!" Cleo exclaimed. "No. Why?"

Max pursed his lips thoughtfully. "I'm an old man, Cleo. With age comes a certain amount of insight. I keep getting the nagging feeling you know more than you're telling me."

Cleo put on her most innocent look, which was hard because she didn't feel innocent at all. "It's about a myth, that's all. I just need some information about how it goes."

The old archaeologist sighed. "All right, Cleo. What myth do you want to know about?"

Cleo pulled the Japanese myth book out of her bag and handed it to him. "It's a Japanese myth, and you're the only guy I know who understands Japanese. I think the story's about a woodcutter named Minokichi and—"

"—and the snow demon, Yuki-onna. Of course I know it." Max had already slipped on his reading glasses and was thumbing through the pages, his face filled with that same intense light her father's face got when he was studying ancient and nearly forgotten things.

"So what happens to Minokichi?" Cleo asked.

Max didn't answer for a moment, his eyes scanning the vertical lines of ideograms from top to bottom. "That's right, that's right," he murmured to himself a few times. "All very interesting." Finally, he looked up and spoke more clearly. "After Minokichi promises not to tell anyone about his meeting with the snow demon, she spares his life."

"Then what?"

"And then it gets really interesting. It turns out the Yuki-onna falls in love with Minokichi. She comes to him in the form of a beautiful young woman—"

"Oh my God," Cleo whispered despite herself. "Yuki . . ."

Max raised an eyebrow. "Cleo, I thought you said you didn't know this myth."

"Please go on," she urged.

"Anyway, Minokichi marries Yuki. They have children."

"What happens to *him*?" Cleo asked pleadingly.

"Well, one day Minokichi makes the mistake of telling his wife the story of what happened with Yuki-onna—"

"Oh my God!" Cleo spun her wheelchair around expertly and rolled toward the door. "Thanks, Max. I've got to go."

"Cleo!" Max was on his feet, sprinting after her. They reached the door at the same time, and Max held it closed. "You found it, didn't you?"

Cleo bit her lip. She had no time for this. Her brother was in danger.

But Max pressed her. "There's more going on here than a project."

"Please," Cleo said, "I have to get back. Right now."

"Cleo, you can tell me. I can help."

Cleo felt her throat tighten up. She shouldn't tell him. Their mythquests were already too hard to keep secret. But Alex was in danger. At any moment the Yuki-onna might attack him. It would take longer to argue with Max than it would to tell him the story.

Finally, she blurted out, "You're not going to believe me. It has to do with the Cyber-Museum. Something happened to it the night Dad disappeared." Max fell into an eager silence, waiting for more. "We think Dad entered a portal," Cleo went on. "And we think the stone had something to do with it."

Max waited for more, but Cleo stopped.

Max's eyes went wide in amazement and disbelief. "Entered a portal?"

"The computer is a gateway to a world of myths," Cleo said.

Max looked bewildered. She might as well have told him they'd discovered that their father was actually from another planet. "Cleo, that's not possible."

Cleo laughed a miserable laugh. "My definition of impossible changed a while ago. I'm not lying. We've gone in looking for him. Each of the objects in the museum lets you enter the myth associated with that object." She willed him to believe her. "Alex is in there right now."

Max was stunned. His confident air of scholarship was gone, replaced by dizzy disbelief. "Oh my God . . . to be inside a myth . . . that's why all the questions about Minokichi."

"And that's why I've got to get back."

Suddenly, she grabbed the door handle and threw the door open wide, wheeling her chair out before the startled archaeologist could react. By the time Max had recovered his wits, Cleo was gone.

Chapter Fourteen

Alex tested his ax against the trunk of a tree.
The *thunk* it made against the wood was solid and
sure. He'd never chopped down a tree before,
but somehow it felt natural. He was starting to
feel very much at home in this myth. He had
slept through the night—at least, it felt like a full
night to him; he had no idea how much time had
passed in the real world. Then he'd eaten break-
fast with his wife and his children and decided to
take a brisk walk in the woods.

Alex was walking on a forest path when

something caught his eye in a stand of trees. He stopped short.

Alex saw a body hanging on the low branches of a tree. He approached the body slowly. "Hello?" he asked timidly. "You okay?"

No response.

As Alex got closer he saw old, gnarled hands and a wizened face twisted into a look of horror.

Noriko. Or rather, Noriko's body.

Noriko's face was ghostly pale and fixed in a look of sheer terror. Her skin was icy.

"Alex!"

Cleo's voice exploded in his ear so loudly that his heart almost stopped.

"Geez! Don't do that!" he yelled back.

There was a pause, and then Cleo said, "She's dead."

"She was right," Alex said. "The snow demon is still out there."

"She was right about more than that, Alex," Cleo said. "I talked to Max Asher. He knows the Minokichi myth."

"And?"

"And he said the snow demon took a human form and married Minokichi. Yuki is the snow demon, Alex!"

Alex reacted as if she'd slapped him. "What? That's crazy."

At their father's desk, Cleo watched Alex on the monitor. She was desperate to get him out of there, but she didn't know how. And what frightened her more was that he didn't seem to want to leave. "Alex, it's not crazy. Think about it. Noriko warned you about her, and now she's dead."

"That doesn't mean it was Yuki."

"I don't believe this," Cleo groaned. "Mom said guys can get stupid over a girl, but this is ridiculous."

Alex stood up and turned away from the body. He couldn't bear to look at Noriko any longer. First he'd watched her husband die, and now she was dead too.

"Alex!" Cleo said. "You know how this happened!"

"It was the snow demon. But that doesn't mean it was Yuki."

Cleo was losing patience. Her brother had totally lost himself in this myth, and she felt helpless. At the moment, she was nothing but a disembodied voice to him, less real than the mythological beings around him.

"Then prove it to yourself," she challenged. "Break the promise you made to her. Tell Yuki the story about how the snow demon spared you. See what happens."

Alex stiffened a bit, annoyed by Cleo's boldness. "And if it's not her, then what?"

Cleo sighed, exasperated. "Alex, it's her. You know it is."

She saw his shoulders slump. He sat down on the path and began to pick at the leaves of a small bush. Finally he said quietly, "Clo, I'm happy here. I think I really love her."

He confessed it as though it were a secret, but Cleo was not surprised. She'd watched him through the monitor. She'd seen the way he looked at the Japanese girl. It was love. But love did not change their circumstances. Alex's life was in danger, and she had no time to be gentle. "Alex, remember, this is not real! It's a myth. And the woman you think you love is a demon."

Alex plucked another leaf off the bush. "Maybe if I don't tell her, I can control her—you know, keep her as Yuki."

"What, like you controlled her when she killed Noriko?" Cleo snapped. She bit her lip. *That's not fair,* she thought. *He deserves better than that.*

"Alex," she said, changing her tactic. "Think about what's been happening around you. You have to come home."

Alex didn't answer, and Cleo realized she'd chosen the wrong argument. He wasn't in this for himself any more than Cleo was. Asking him to think of his own life wouldn't sway him.

"You know what you have to do, Alex," she whispered. "If you're not going to do it for yourself, do it for Dad."

Chapter Fifteen

Alex dragged his feet through the door of his cottage. His head hung low, and he felt cold, although Yuki had built a warm fire in the house. The children lay in one corner of the room, dozing in an afternoon nap. Yuki herself was sitting beside the fire sewing. She smiled at him with a warmth all her own.

"You're home so soon. Don't tell me the forest has run out of trees," she said with a laugh.

Alex stood in the center of the room, bracing himself. For a moment he couldn't speak. Finally, he forced the words from his lips. "I found Noriko. In the woods."

Yuki frowned. "What do you mean? Was she hurt?"

"You know what I mean."

Yuki stopped sewing. Her eyes grew wide, and there was a hint of panic and anger in them, as though Alex had just threatened to tear away her entire life.

"I . . . I don't know," she protested.

Alex shook his head. "Her blood was gone, Yuki. She was murdered." He couldn't bring himself to say what needed to be said . . . that he knew who the murderer was.

"It doesn't have anything to do with us!" Yuki said sharply. Her voice cracked with desperate emotion. "Minokichi, I beg you. Put it out of your mind. Think of our happy life!"

Alex turned away, unable to look at her any longer. The anguish on her face matched the feeling of betrayal in his heart. The only thing worse than causing someone pain was knowing beforehand just how much pain you would cause. "I can't, Yuki," he said in a hoarse voice. "You know I can't. A long time ago, when I was just learning to work with wood, I was out on a journey with my master, Mosaku."

Yuki leaped to her feet and ran, as though trying to escape his voice. But she only got as far as the window. She sobbed, covering her ears with her hands. "I don't want to hear this! Please don't tell me!"

Alex grabbed her by the arm and spun her around. There were tears on her cheeks, and he felt his own eyes stinging. "I don't want to tell you, but I have to. That night there was a snow spirit. A demon who came and killed Mosaku right in front of me. She took his—"

"Stop! If you love me, if you love what we have, you'll stop!"

"She let me live," he went on, determined now to finish. Telling the story brought the memory back to life for him. In his mind's eye he saw the kindly old man—at first warm and laughing, as when they'd first met; then cold and lifeless after the appearance of the snow demon. The vision made Alex's task easier. "She let me live," he repeated, "but said I could never tell a soul or she'd kill me the same way."

Yuki winced as if she'd been stung.

Alex gritted his teeth and gripped her arms

with fierce strength. "And I've kept that promise, Yuki. I . . . I've kept that promise for years. But now I can't. I swore I'd never tell. And if you hadn't killed Noriko, maybe I never would have."

Yuki sobbed once, but then her tears stopped flowing, like a river turned suddenly to ice. "I loved you," she said coldly.

"I know," he whispered.

By the time the words had left his mouth, the world was exploding.

A howl split the air, more shrill than a winter wind. The windows shattered, and ice crystals sharper than glass swirled around the room. A brilliant flash of white light blinded Alex, and he staggered backward as a freezing wind struck him, threatening to tear the clothes from his body.

"You broke your word!"

The voice was inhuman. Yuki's sweet voice, the voice that reminded him of birdsong, was gone. This was the voice of the Yuki-onna, hard as winter, deep as a frozen lake, sharp as jagged ice.

Alex, holding one arm before his face against the whirlwind, beheld the snow demon for the second time. She was dressed all in white, with a white face and eyes as colorless as death. A deadly light glowed all around her. On her face was an expression so terrible, it threatened to stop his heart.

"I wanted to trust you!" the demon screamed.

Alex was terrified. Myth or no myth, this was reality for him while he was in the Alterworld. With a thought, this creature could freeze him and drain the last drop of blood from his body. He had the cold, frightening feeling that he beheld his own death.

"I loved you!" he shouted over the storm. "I loved who I thought you were!"

The snow demon hissed, the sound like sleet streaking through broken branches. "I let myself *feel*! I gave a stupid mortal power over me!"

"You loved!" he replied. "There's nothing wrong with that!"

"Love!" The Yuki-onna spat the word out like a curse. "How long have I tried to live on human love, instead of the blood I crave!"

The ice demon moved toward him, her fangs bared. She stretched out her hands, the claws nearly touching his face. Alex felt her breath on his skin, colder even than the snow, and he recoiled in fear.

"The cold was what spawned me," the Yuki-onna moaned, half in anger and half in sorrow. "I should have stayed close to the cold." The creature's eyes bored into him, and a new expression filled her face. Alex recognized the meaning of that look. Hunger.

The Yuki-onna lunged forward. "No!" Alex cried, throwing both arms up to protect himself. The creature pushed his arms aside, and he felt her grab his throat. Her viselike grip slammed him against the wall, and he shut his eyes tight, expecting to feel at any moment the freezing cold bite of the demon.

It never came. After a moment, realizing he was still alive, Alex peeked out from behind his arms. He saw the demon standing there before him. Her hands still gripped his throat. She looked miserable and still angry, but her rage was spent. In its place, he saw disgust.

"You lead a blessed life, Minokichi. I spared you the first time because you made me wish for things I had never dreamed of. Now I spare your life again because of those same feelings. I loved you too much."

The Yuki-onna released her grip on his throat and glided backward, away from him. She looked toward the corner of the room where the children now cowered, too frightened even to cry out.

Alex rubbed his throat, grateful to be able to breathe. "Yuki," he whispered.

The ice demon looked back at him in disdain. "There is no Yuki anymore."

He could see that. The last vestiges of humanity were melting away from her, leaving only the cold heart of the demon. The Yuki-onna drifted toward the door but then turned back to Alex, fixing him with a hard stare.

"I promise you this, Minokichi. If you mistreat my children . . . or speak badly of me to them . . . I will come back. And next time I will destroy you."

The deadly promise in her voice made Alex shudder. He thought of how foolish he had been to think he could control Yuki. Even years later, thinking of her threat, he would shiver as though caught in a snowstorm, and no amount of warmth could comfort him until the memory had passed.

With those words, the ice demon departed.

The figure of the woman collapsed into mist, and the mist swirled around in an icy whirlwind that blew itself out of the cottage. The demon left behind a battered cottage, a terrified man, and two stunned and speechless children shivering with fright.

And something else.

Alex saw it lying on the floor. A small, delicately carved comb. It was the comb Yuki had always used in her hair. The same one he had touched in the CyberMuseum. He walked to it but did not pick it up. He knew what would happen when he touched it.

The two children peeked out from beneath their covers. Seeing that all was quiet, they jumped to their feet and rushed to wrap their arms around him.

"Is she gone?"

Alex stroked their hair to reassure them and soothed them with the only words he could think of. "She's gone," he said sadly. "She's gone."

"Alex."

Cleo's voice broke through the silence after the storm.

"Alex," she said again when he didn't answer. "Touch the comb and get back here."

He looked up into the air. The children followed his gaze, but they saw nothing. And they heard nothing except his answer to Cleo.

"I don't think I can leave them," he said. "They're my kids."

"They're Minokichi's kids, Alex. If the myth survives after you leave, it'll survive with Minokichi in your place, just like you were in his."

"Do we know that?" he protested.

"We don't know anything . . . except that you don't belong there. They'll be all right. They'll be with their father."

Their father. Cleo's words struck home. He realized he would envy these children, even if they only existed in the Alterworld. They would have their father with them.

"Everything's going to be okay now," he said to them in his steadiest voice. "Go back to bed now.

"Your mom," he went on, "she loved you a lot. And so do I."

The children smiled at him, confused but happy, and crawled back under their covers. As they did, Alex reached down and picked up the comb.

Chapter Sixteen

An instant later, Alex was standing in the study in the Bellows house. Dizziness overcame him, and he fell to his knees. He shook his head, clearing away the shock and terror of the demon's visitation. When he was finally able to look up, he found Cleo looking down at him sympathetically.

"I'm sorry," she said.

Alex nodded. Instead of getting up, he lay back on the floor, staring up at the ceiling. Now that he was out of the myth, he realized how happy he was to be home. To be in the real world. Still, the memories of his quest lingered with him, and he shook his head.

"You think you know somebody. Next thing, you don't know *what* you know. . . ."

Cleo held out the Japanese myth book. "Does it help that in the myth, Minokichi turns out to be a great father—and his kids are never abandoned?"

Alex thought about it. "Yes, it does help."

"Good," she said. "Because things have been going on out here that are really getting complicated."

Alex sat up, suddenly alert. He'd been so wrapped up in his own problems, he'd forgotten about Cleo's. "What? Tell me."

"I didn't have any choice," his sister said, starting in the middle of her story. "I needed to find out about the myth, and I thought I could ask Max—"

"Cleo!"

"I know, I know!" she shot back, stopping his protest before it could begin. "But I thought he wouldn't figure out why I was asking, and then he did figure it out. I mean, how could that be? *I* don't even believe what we're doing half the time; how could he guess it? But he did. And then I had to tell him what was going on, and—"

"Stop!" Alex said, holding up one hand. "You're not making any sense. What did you tell him?"

Cleo bit her lip. "About the Cyber-Museum . . . and what we're doing."

For Alex, it had been almost a lifetime since he'd been in the real world, and all he wanted to do was rest. But there was no time. He and Cleo sped over to Max Asher's house and nearly pushed their way through his front door. Alex found himself rambling on, with Cleo jumping in whenever she could, as he sought to explain away everything Cleo had said.

"So you see," he was saying, "it's been really hard for Cleo to deal with all this about Dad—and she's started making stuff up—"

Max held up both hands, cutting off his speech. When Alex stopped talking, the old archaeologist shook his head. He looked from Alex to Cleo and back to Alex, his eyes flashing with anger.

"Alex, this isn't a game," Max said, his voice fearful. "I know what happened to your father. And I know what you've been doing."

Alex opened his mouth to spin a new web of lies. But he stopped. He hated telling lies in the first place, and right now he didn't have the energy to come up with a good one.

"Okay, Max, you know. But we'd really appreciate it if you could kind of keep it to yourself."

As Max looked at them, Cleo and Alex could see the sense of urgency in his eyes. "You don't really know how dangerous this is, do you?"

Alex thought of the snow demon with her razor-sharp claws around his throat. "We have a pretty good idea."

The archaeologist nodded. "Then if you want to get your father back, you're going to need help."

Cleo was surprised, nervous, and excited. "You'll help us?"

"Not only will I help you, I can connect you with others who can help too. If your father really has freed Gorgos, it's going to be a difficult task to get him back inside the stone. We're going to need all the help we can get."

Alex and Cleo both felt a sudden surge of hope. But just as quickly as it arose, it subsided as the older man's face darkened in concern. "Unfortunately," he added thoughtfully, "there are also those who would do anything to get their hands on it."

"For the money?" Cleo asked.

Max grunted. "For the power. Who knows what powers one would have if one were able to enter the myths that shaped our cultures and rewrite them?"

Alex waved a hand impatiently. "Max, finding the stone is one thing, but—"

"You want to know if we can find your father," Max said. "I don't know any more than you do. But I'm an optimist."

He smiled at them both. "The one thing I do know is that we won't give up. If he's in there somewhere, we'll do everything we can to get him back. Now let's get to work."

The Myth of Minokichi

According to ancient Japanese legend, two woodcutters, Mosaku, an old man, and Minokichi, his apprentice, lived in Musashi Province. They worked in the woods across a river from their home. One night, they were traveling home when a snowstorm crossed their path. They reached the river, but the ferry was on the other side and couldn't take them back. So they took shelter in the ferryman's hut. In time, the two fell asleep while the storm raged outside.

Minokichi awoke to snow falling in his face. The door of the hut was open, and a woman in white was leaning over Mosaku, blowing white air into his face. She then turned to Minokichi and said, "I intended to treat you like the other man. But I cannot help feeling some pity for you, because you are so young. . . . You are a pretty boy, Minokichi, and I will not hurt you now. But if you ever tell anybody—even your own mother—about what you have seen this night, I will know it, and then I will kill you. . . . Remember what I say!"

After she had left, Minokichi ran to Mosaku and touched his face, finding it as cold as ice. His dear friend and mentor was dead.

The next day, the ferryman found Minokichi lying next to Mosaku. Minokichi was ill for some time but eventually recovered and returned to work cutting wood. One day while he was on his way home, he came across a very beautiful girl named O-Yuki. She was on her way to Yedo to meet relatives who might be able to help find her a position as a servant. She and Minokichi took a liking to each other, and he convinced her to stay at his house for a while. Minokichi's mother liked O-Yuki as well and asked her to delay her trip for some time. O-Yuki never made her trip to Yedo but remained and became Minokichi's wife.

Yuki was a wonderful wife. She helped Minokichi through the death of his mother and bore him ten children. Even after all this, she still looked as young as the day he met her. One evening, as he was watching her sew, he told her that she reminded him of the woman in white he had seen those many years ago. "Asleep or awake, that was the only time I saw a being as beautiful as you. Of course, she was not a human being, and I was afraid of her, very much afraid, but she was so white . . . Indeed, I have never been sure whether it was a dream that I saw, or the Woman of the Snow."

Then, suddenly, Yuki sprang up and said, "It was I—I—I! And I told you I would kill you if you ever said one word about it! But for those children asleep there, I would kill you this moment! And now you had better take very, very good care of them, for if they ever have a reason to complain of you, I will treat you as you deserve!" Then she melted into a white cloud and disappeared, never to be seen again.